## Put Beginning Readers on the Right Track with ALL ABOARD READING™

The All Aboard Reading series is especially for beginning readers. Written by noted authors and illustrated in full color, these are books that children really and truly *want* to read—books to excite their imagination, tickle their funny bone, expand their interests, and support their feelings. With four different reading levels, All Aboard Reading lets you choose which books are most appropriate for your children and their growing abilities.

**Picture Readers—for Ages 3 to 6**
Picture Readers have super-simple texts with many nouns appearing as rebus pictures. At the end of each book are 24 flash cards—on one side is the rebus picture; on the other side is the written-out word.

**Level 1—for Preschool through First Grade Children**
Level 1 books have very few lines per page, very large type, easy words, lots of repetition, and pictures with visual "cues" to help children figure out the words on the page.

**Level 2—for First Grade to Third Grade Children**
Level 2 books are printed in slightly smaller type than Level 1 books. The stories are more complex, but there is still lots of repetition in the text and many pictures. The sentences are quite simple and are broken up into short lines to make reading easier.

**Level 3—for Second Grade through Third Grade Children**
Level 3 books have considerably longer texts, use harder words and more complicated sentences.

All Aboard for happy reading!

To Reed—S.A.K.

To Scott, Jamie, Chris
and Brandon—J.C.

Photo credits: pp. 15 and back cover, 26, 37, and 48, AP/Wide World Photos.

*Library of Congress Cataloging-in-Publication Data*

Kramer, Sydelle.
    Football stars / by S. A. Kramer ; illustrated by Jim Campbell.
       p.    cm.—(All aboard reading)
    "Level 3, grades 2-3."
    Summary: profiles four star players in the National Football League: Deion Sanders, Barry Sanders, Jerry Rice, and Troy Aikman. 1. Football players—United States—Biography—Juvenile literature.  [1. Football players.]  I. Campbell, Jim, 1942-  ill.
    II. Title. III. Series.
    GV939.A1K73  1997
    796.332'64'0922—dc21
    [B]                                         96-37530
                                                                   CIP
                                                                    AC

ISBN 0-448-41700-6 (GB)   A B C D E F G H I J

ISBN 0-448-41591-7 (pbk)   A B C D E F G H I J

**ALL
ABOARD
READING**™

Level 3
Grades 2-3

# FOOTBALL STARS

### By S. A. Kramer
### Illustrated by Jim Campbell

### With photographs

Grosset & Dunlap • New York

## Top-Dollar Man

October 16, 1994. The San Francisco 49ers are in Atlanta to play the Falcons. They're tied for the division title. Which is the better team?

Deion Sanders thinks he knows. Last year he played for the Falcons. Right now he's a 49er. The NFL's top cornerback, he's sure of himself. He feels whichever team he's on is the one with the edge.

4

Deion's the best there is against the long pass. Receivers hate when he covers them. Quarterbacks are afraid to throw near him. At six-foot-one, 190 pounds, he's strong and quick. Cutting and running, he can change direction in a flash.

Deion is tricky. Sometimes he slows down so his man thinks he's in the clear. Then watch out! The pass goes up, and Deion speeds by him. He's not trying for the tackle—he's going for the ball.

Now the first half is almost over. The 49ers are in the lead. But the Falcons are close to scoring.

If they get a touchdown, it's anyone's game. Deion decides to show his old team what he can do.

He lines up across from the wide receiver. He's crouched like a lion, ready to pounce. His arms hang down at his sides. His fingers wiggle. He can't wait to attack.

The ball is snapped. Deion explodes
off the line. The pass spins toward the
wide receiver. But Deion is there! He steps
in front of his man and grabs the ball.

Heading up the sidelines, he doesn't
look especially fast. But not one of the
Falcons can keep up. Deion may be the
fastest man in the game.

He races by the Atlanta bench. His old teammates are watching. Suddenly he starts teasing them, shouting and flashing his biggest grin.

At full speed, he lifts his legs as if he's marching in a band. It's Deion's way of telling the Atlanta Falcons that the game is over.

He runs 93 yards. Touchdown! With his hands in the air, he does a little dance in the end zone. More than 60,000 Falcon fans boo, then boo some more. Deion just smiles and keeps dancing.

He has broken the game wide open. Now the Falcons don't have a chance. The 49ers end up winning, 42-3. With Deion's help, they go on to win the Super Bowl. He is named the 1994 Defensive Player of the Year.

In 1995, Deion joins the Dallas Cowboys. There, he becomes one of the few men in many years to play both offense and defense. Nicknamed Prime Time, he wins another Super Bowl ring. Some experts call him football's most exciting player.

He certainly is the flashiest. Twelve
thick gold chains hang from his neck.
From them dangle crosses, dollar signs,
and his number, all in diamonds. He
wears three gold watches and two gold
rings. There's a gold cap on one tooth,
and a diamond earring in each ear.

Money matters to Deion. Under his uniform, he wears his lucky green boxer shorts with gold dollar signs. He's so pleased he's rich, he signs his name "Deion $anders."

He's never forgotten what it's like to be poor. He was raised in a Florida housing project. His father, a drug user, was never around. He left home soon after Deion was born.

His mother worked, but couldn't afford a baby-sitter. From the age of seven, Deion took care of himself. He dressed and ate alone, and got himself to school.

In high school Deion was a top athlete. He hoped that sports would lead him to a better life. It did. After a great college career at Florida State, he joined the NFL in 1989.

Deion also plays major-league baseball. He's the only man ever to appear in a World Series <u>and</u> a Super Bowl. No other pro has hit a home run and scored a touchdown in the same week.

Yet Deion isn't popular with everyone. Some fans say he does nothing but brag. A few complain he won't make tackles because he might get his uniform dirty. They call him Neon Deion, and it's not a compliment.

It's true Deion shows off. But fans don't see him behind the scenes. That's when he shows his serious side. He works very hard. One coach says "he studies and studies" other teams' moves.

His teammates rely on him. His energy gets them going. When he clowns around in the locker room, it helps them relax.

Fans aren't certain who the real Deion is. But one thing is for sure—he's one of football's most exciting stars.

## Barryball

December 24, 1989. It's the last game of the season. Only a minute to go. The Detroit Lions lead the Atlanta Falcons, and the Lions have the ball. But fans in the stadium aren't thinking about the score. They're wondering if Barry Sanders can win the NFL rushing title today.

The Lions star running back, 21-year-old Barry is just a rookie. But he's already gained 158 yards in this game, and 1,470 for the year. He needs only ten more to finish first. Ten yards should be a snap for Barry.

He's like a human pinball, bouncing off tackles and bursting through the line. In the blink of an eye, he can stop short, then start. Running left, then right, then left, he zigzags downfield. No one knows where he'll go next—not even Barry.

He's so hard to tackle, the Minnesota Vikings once said he was cheating. They thought Barry had sprayed a chemical on his uniform to make it slippery. But his uniform was clean. It was his moves and fakes that got him past the Vikings.

Now his coach comes up to Barry on the sidelines. "Do you want to go in?" he asks. Everyone thinks Barry will say yes.

After all, it's his last chance to earn the title.

But Barry says, "Coach, let's just win it and go home." The fans are amazed that he stays on the bench. Later he explains, "When everyone is out for statistics . . . that's when trouble starts." Barry feels the team comes first. What <u>he</u> does just isn't as important.

Barry believes showing off is wrong. To him, doing the right thing is what makes life worth living. He doesn't need to be a sports hero to feel good about himself.

Barry doesn't win the rushing title. But he's named Offensive Rookie of the Year. He says he couldn't have done it without his linemen. To show his thanks, he gives each a $10,000 watch.

The very next year, Barry does win the title. Then, in 1991, he's named Most Valuable Player. In 1994, he's Offensive Player of the Year. By 1996, he's become one of the top ten rushers of all time.

When Barry was young, no one could have guessed that he would be a football star. He started playing at age nine, but he says, "I was always smaller than most kids." To make up for his size, he acted like a bully. He even stole candy and threw rocks at passing cars.

In ninth grade, he was only five feet tall and 100 pounds. His football coach was afraid to play him—he thought Barry would get hurt. But Barry's father talked the coach into giving his son a chance.

Barry came through. He played well in high school. But because of his size, he had trouble making a college team. Finally, Oklahoma State took him and Barry showed what he could do. He set twenty-four records, winning the 1988 Heisman Trophy for best college player of the year.

By now Barry was five-foot-eight, 203 pounds. Yet many experts felt he was too small for the NFL. Barry knew they were wrong. He was sure he could play against big athletes. Over the years, he'd made himself into one of football's strongest men.

Lifting weights had made his legs powerful—his thighs were more than three feet around! He could jump 41½ inches straight into the air. Working out with 600-pound weights was easy for him.

The Lions decided to give Barry a chance. They made him their back. Barry didn't let them down. He became a Hall of Fame shoo-in. Now when he's on the field, no one thinks about his size.

Barry's greatest football dream is to
win the Super Bowl. But there's something
even more important to him—his family.

He was raised in Kansas with ten
brothers and sisters. His parents were
poor, so their house was small. All thirteen
people in the family shared three bedrooms.

The Sanders family has stayed close over the years. Barry won't make big decisions without their help. He wouldn't leave college for the NFL until he got his family's advice.

His religion is also important to him. Ten percent of all he earns goes to his church. He often studies the Bible, and quotes from it to fans.

A quiet guy, Barry stays out of the spotlight. But his talent shines through.

## Mr. 49er

Crawford, Mississippi, 1978. Sixteen-year-old Jerry Rice is cutting a class. He is sneaking down his high-school hall, when someone taps him on the shoulder. Jerry wheels around. It's the assistant principal!

Jerry panics. He takes off like he's been shot from a cannon. The assistant principal can't believe his eyes. Jerry is <u>fast</u>!

But he's finally caught. He gets six whacks with a leather strap. And his punishment isn't over. Either Jerry stays after school—or he tries out for football. The assistant principal knows that the team needs a good runner.

Jerry doesn't like football. But being stuck after school is worse. He makes the team easily. His mom isn't happy. She's afraid he might get hurt. Jerry plays anyway. It turns out football is fun! And being a receiver is easy. Without knowing it, he's been practicing for years.

Every summer Jerry works for his
father. He stands on a high platform and
his brother throws four bricks at a time up
to him. Jerry catches all four every time.

Grabbing bricks makes his hands tough
and fast. Running gets his legs strong. His
high school is five miles from home.
There's no bus—he jogs to school and
back.

Now that he's on the team, Jerry practices all the time. No matter how bad the throw, Jerry tries to catch it. One time the ball shoots over a briar patch. Jerry grabs it—and falls in. When he climbs out he's covered with scratches—but he still has the ball.

Jerry's so good at football, he can play five different positions. But when he gets to the state university, he's named wide receiver. He sets eighteen college records, and joins the San Francisco 49ers in 1985.

In high school, football was Jerry's punishment. After college, it becomes the most important thing in his life. But some experts insist that he will never be a star. They say he is fast for a college team, but slow for the NFL.

Jerry's nervous. He wants to prove himself right away. But the pressure is too much for him. In his first eleven games, he drops eleven passes. Sometimes he forgets what play he's supposed to run. Fans boo him so loudly in one game that he cries.

But after a while, Jerry settles down. In the season's last games, he shows he's got what it takes to make it. By timing

bursts of speed just right, he shoots past
defenders. Other players slow down to
catch a pass, but Jerry grabs it without
braking.

He never seems to tire or get tackled too hard. With his great balance and long fingers, he scoops up balls at his ankles. Always thinking about the end zone, he turns short gains into touchdowns.

Each year Jerry gets better. By 1987, he's breaking records. That's when he scores the most touchdowns ever (22) in a single season.

His powerful body helps make him the NFL's most feared receiver. Even off-season, Jerry trains five hours a day, six days a week. Six-foot-two, 193 pounds, he lifts weights and runs up mountains. He's out exercising even in the rain.

The experts all say Jerry's sure to make the Hall of Fame. Yet he still feels he has to prove himself every year in every game. Sometimes he doubts his talent. He can't sleep for days before a big game. Jerry says he can't relax.

But when it's time to take the field, he's suddenly calm. If the game's on the line, he wants the ball. A deep threat on every play, he manages to stay open even when three men are covering him.

In all of football history, no one has caught more passes, gained more receiving yards, or scored more touchdowns than Jerry. He's proud to have won four Super Bowl rings. Everyone agrees that Jerry Rice is the greatest receiver ever.

## America's Quarterback

Phoenix, Arizona. October 23, 1994. The Dallas Cowboys are facing the Arizona Cardinals. It's only the first quarter of the game. But the Cowboys are sure they're going to win. After all, superstar Troy Aikman is their quarterback.

With his strong arm and quick release, Troy's passes are as fast as bullets. He can zing bull's-eyes to receivers surrounded by defenders. Not even hard-rushing tacklers can hurry Troy into a bad throw.

He's the most patient quarterback in the NFL. To get a good pass off, he stands his ground, even if he's going to get clobbered. Troy almost never dumps the ball just to avoid a sack.

But being patient means he takes a lot of hits. Often hurt, he has aching knees, a sore elbow, and a bad back. He doesn't complain, though. He is used to living with pain.

Troy was born with twisted feet that had to be fixed. He was only eight months old when casts were put on both legs. Until he was three, he wore special shoes. At night his heels were strapped together. He learned early how to be tough.

Today he'll need every bit of that toughness. The Cowboys drive to the nine-yard line. It's first and goal to go.

Troy wants to pass for a touchdown, but no one is open. Suddenly he sees the Cardinal linebacker charging toward him! There's just one way to dodge the tackle—scramble to the left.

On the move, Troy tries to throw. But the linebacker's already on top of him. The defender's helmet smashes his chin. Troy goes down hard. His head slams to the ground. Is he hurt again?

Troy gets up. He goes to the huddle. There's a ringing sound in his head. Blood gushes from his mouth and chin. The Cowboys are worried. They stand and stare at him.

Troy's head hurts. He's bitten his tongue. His chin is split open. But right now he doesn't care.

He glares at his teammates. His blue eyes are hard. To him, there's only one thing that counts—scoring a touchdown. Troy wants to win. Even if he's hurt, he's got to give his best.

It's no different today. Troy won't leave the game until the Cowboys score. Two plays later, he throws a perfect touchdown pass. The Cowboys take the lead. Now he can sit down.

As soon as Troy is on the sidelines, he starts to feel strange. He needs six stitches in his chin. Even worse, he has what's called a concussion. When his head hit the ground, the blow smacked his brain against his skull. It's his second one this year.

Troy is in a daze. He has to leave the game. But he's made sure the Cowboys are ahead. They go on to win, 28-21.

The next week he's back. All his teammates are relieved. Troy puts a lot of pressure on himself. He sets high standards for his team. If a Cowboy makes a mistake, Troy yells at him. But none of that matters. Troy is the Cowboys' leader.

He's come a long way from Henryetta, Oklahoma. His family moved to a ranch there when he was twelve. At first he hated the place. It wasn't like California, where he was born. There wasn't a McDonald's or a mall. The dirt roads were so rough, Troy couldn't even ride his bike.

Every day he had chores to do. He got up early to feed the pigs. At night he hauled hay from the fields. But slowly he began to enjoy his new life.

Then, in high school, Troy discovered football. A talented athlete, he quickly became a star. Troy didn't always fit his classmates' idea of a sports hero. But that never stopped him from doing what he wanted.

His friends found that out when he signed up for typing class. Typing was only for girls, they said. Troy didn't care. He was the only boy in a class of thirty-eight girls. That year he won the typing prize!

Troy went on to UCLA. He became the best college quarterback in the country. But when he joined the NFL in 1989, he suddenly flopped. A rookie with the Cowboys, he started eleven games—and lost all of them. He had the league's worst quarterback rating.

Troy was so upset, he thought about quitting. But he stuck it out with the Cowboys. In his second season, he finally won his first game. Every year, he and the team got better. Now experts feel that Troy is one of the best in the NFL.

He's the second highest-rated quarterback in playoff history. No one has completed a higher percentage of playoff passes. He's one of only three quarterbacks to win three or more Super Bowls.

But for Troy, Super Bowl stardom isn't everything. No matter what, he has to do what he feels is right. Troy's the real thing on and off the field.